ULTIMATE STICKER BOOK

Disney · PIXAR

INCREDIBLES 2

How to use this book

Read the captions, then find the sticker that best fits the space.
(Hint: check the sticker labels for clues!)

There are lots of fantastic extra stickers too!

DK | Penguin Random House

Written and edited by Julia March
Senior Designer Lynne Moulding

First American Edition, 2018
Published in the United States by DK Publishing
345 Hudson Street, New York, New York 10014

Page design copyright © 2018 Dorling Kindersley Limited
DK, a Division of Penguin Random House LLC
18 19 20 21 22 10 9 8 7 6 5 4 3 2 1
001–307595–May/2018

Published in Great Britain by Dorling Kindersley Limited.

A catalog record for this book is available from the Library of Congress.
ISBN: 978-1-4654-6689-1

DK books are available at special discounts when purchased in bulk
for sales promotions, premiums, fund-raising, or educational use.
For details, contact: DK Publishing Special Markets,
345 Hudson Street, New York, New York 10014
SpecialSales@dk.com

Printed and bound in China

A WORLD OF IDEAS:
SEE ALL THERE IS TO KNOW

www.dk.com
www.disney.com

INCREDIBLE FAMILY

When danger looms, the Parr family become an amazing Superhero team named the Incredibles. Sadly, the Incredibles' crime-fighting days might be over. The government says Supers cause too much chaos. It is illegal to be a Super!

SUPER FAMILY
Mr. Incredible is strong and Elastigirl is stretchy. Their son Dash is fast, and Violet, their daughter, can vanish.

MR. INCREDIBLE
Bob Parr is Mr. Incredible. He is one of the strongest Supers in the world. He can punch through brick walls!

ELASTIGIRL
Helen Parr is often stretched to the limit, both as a mom and as the incredible Elastigirl.

JACK-JACK
Jack-Jack is the youngest member of the Parr family. Nobody knows whether he has any powers... yet!

© Disney/Pixar

© Disney/Pixar

SECRET SCHEME
Helen and Bob hear of a billionaire's scheme to get Supers re-legalized. Will they sign up?

SUPER NEW ROLES

Helen and Bob join the scheme to get Supers legalized. Bob is slightly miffed when Elastigirl is chosen for the first mission. It means she will be living away from home for a while. He isn't used to being a stay-at-home dad!

© Disney/Pixar

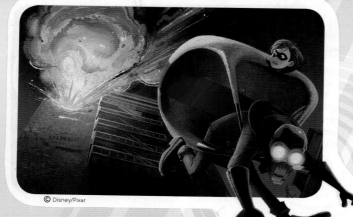

© Disney/Pixar

TEMPORARY SPLIT
Bob and Helen are a little worried about living apart. The Incredibles have never been split up before.

SKY DIVE
When a villain she is chasing jumps out of a window, Elastigirl stretches into a parachute shape and follows!

RISKY RESCUES
Elastigirl performs many risky rescues and fearless feats. If she does well, the government might agree to legalize Supers again.

TOUGH JOB
Mr. Incredible can withstand bullets and blows. But can he withstand three boisterous kids?

© Disney/Pixar

© Disney/Pixar

LUXURY PAD
The billionaire offers Bob, Violet, and Dash the use of a luxury mansion. It's an architectural wonder!

BABY BONDING
Bob has lots of time to bond with Jack-Jack while the older kids are at school.

ELASTICYCLE
Elastigirl is thrilled with her new costume and her new vehicle. The Elasticycle is fast enough to outpace a speeding train.

5

INCREDIBLE KIDS

When Helen calls Bob, he says he is doing fine running the house. In fact, he is barely finding time to run a faucet. It's the kids! Dash and Violet have problems they need help with, and Jack-Jack is behaving a little strangely.

© Disney/Pixar

DASH
Dash is so fast that he can run across water. No one knows his top speed. It's too fast to time!

CRINGE!
Bob takes the kids to a restaurant where Violet's crush works. Violet cringes with embarrassment!

VIOLET
As well as her ability to disappear, Violet has the power to create protective force fields.

MATH HASSLE
Bob struggles to help Dash with his homework. He hasn't had to do equations since his own school days!

VIOLET VS. VOYD

With neither parent around, Violet must battle a hypnotized Super named Voyd on her own.

INCREDIBLY CUTE

Jack-Jack may or may not have superpowers, but one thing is for sure, he is a super-cute baby!

GETTING ALONG

At least Violet and Dash are getting along these days. Dash rarely takes his teasing too far.

JACK-JACK

Lately, Jack-Jack has started doing things that other babies don't. Things like shooting beams from his eyes and multiplying. He is clearly going to be as incredible as the rest of his family!

BABY SUIT

Jack-Jack now has a Supersuit like all the other Incredibles. His has room for a diaper underneath!

PROUD DAD

Mr. Incredible is thrilled (but a litt' nervous) about baby's new powers.

S

Ja
ra
ro
new